For my wife Joanne

Copyright © 1991 by Kenn Compton
Printed in the United States of America
First Edition

Library of Congress Cataloging-in-Publication Data
Compton, Kenn.
Happy Christmas to all! / written and illustrated by Kenn Compton.
p.   cm.
Summary: Santa gets a surprise when he arrives home after making
his Christmas rounds.
ISBN 0-8234-0890-6
[1. Santa Claus—Fiction.   2. Christmas—Fiction.]   I. Title.
PZ7.C7364Hap   1991   90-29078   CIP   AC
[E]—dc20

HAPPY CHRISTMAS TO ALL!

written and illustrated by

KENN COMPTON

Holiday House / New York

AT LEAST YOU
WAITED UP FOR
ME, DIDN'T YOU,
SNOWBALL.